SPORTS ALL-STARS

JOE BURROW

Jon M. Fishman

Lerner Publications ◆ Minneapolis

SCORE BIG with sports fans, reluctant readers, and report writers!

Lerner Sports is a database of high-interest biographies profiling notable sports superstars. Packed with fascinating facts, these bios explore the backgrounds, career-defining moments, and everyday lives of popular athletes. Lerner Sports is perfect for young readers developing research skills or looking for exciting sports content.

LERNER SPORTS FEATURES:
- Keyword search
- Topic navigation menus
- Fast facts
- Related bio suggestions to encourage more reading
- Admin view of reader statistics
- Fresh content updated regularly

and more!

Visit **LernerSports.com** for a free trial!

Copyright © 2022 by Lerner Publishing Group, Inc.

All rights reserved. International copyright secured. No part of this book may be reproduced, stored in a retrieval system, or transmitted in any form or by any means—electronic, mechanical, photocopying, recording, or otherwise—without the prior written permission of Lerner Publishing Group, Inc., except for the inclusion of brief quotations in an acknowledged review.

Lerner Publications Company
An imprint of Lerner Publishing Group, Inc.
241 First Avenue North
Minneapolis, MN 55401 USA

For reading levels and more information, look up this title at www.lernerbooks.com.

Main body text set in Albany Std. Typeface provided by Agfa.

Library of Congress Cataloging-in-Publication Data

Names: Fishman, Jon M., author.
Title: Joe Burrow / Jon M. Fishman.
Description: Minneapolis : Lerner Publications, [2022] | Series: Sports all-stars (Lerner sports) | Includes bibliographical references and index. | Audience: Ages 7–11 | Audience: Grades 4–6 | Summary: "Quarterback Joe Burrow was the Cincinnati Bengals' star pick in the 2020 NFL Draft. Learn about Burrow's stellar college career, his workout routine, and how he stays connected to his hometown"— Provided by publisher.
Identifiers: LCCN 2021004197 (print) | LCCN 2021004198 (ebook) | ISBN 9781728404349 (library binding) | ISBN 9781728423142 (paperback) | ISBN 9781728418803 (ebook)
Subjects: LCSH: Burrow, Joe, 1996—-Juvenile literature. | Football players—United States—Biography—Juvenile literature. | Quarterbacks (Football)—United States—Biography—Juvenile literature.
Classification: LCC GV939.B873 F57 2022 (print) | LCC GV939.B873 (ebook) | DDC 796.332092 [B]—dc23

LC record available at https://lccn.loc.gov/2021004197
LC ebook record available at https://lccn.loc.gov/2021004198

Manufactured in the United States of America
1-48492-49006-4/14/2021

TABLE OF CONTENTS

Whatever It Takes 4

Facts at a Glance 5

Joe Cool 8

Time to Work 15

Fighting Hunger 20

Time to Heal 24

All-Star Stats 28

Glossary 29

Source Notes 30

Learn More 31

Index 32

WHATEVER IT TAKES

The Cincinnati Bengals were a losing team. In 2019, they lost 14 games and won only two. That was the worst record in the National Football League (NFL). The team and its fans

Joe Burrow throws a pass in a game against the Philadelphia Eagles.

FACTS AT A GLANCE

- **Date of birth:** December 10, 1996

- **Position:** quarterback

- **League:** NFL

- **Professional highlights:** threw 60 touchdown passes in a college football season; was selected by the Cincinnati Bengals with the first overall pick in the NFL Draft; suffered a serious knee injury in his 10th NFL game

- **Personal highlights:** played football and basketball in high school; loves *SpongeBob SquarePants*; helped start the Joe Burrow Hunger Relief Fund

Burrow scored his first NFL touchdown against the Chargers in September 2020.

hoped their new quarterback, Joe Burrow, could lead the Bengals to victory.

Burrow's first game with Cincinnati was against the Los Angeles Chargers on September 13, 2020. In the first quarter, Burrow took the ball. Instead of looking for a teammate to throw it to, he took off running. He charged up the middle of the field for a 23-yard touchdown.

Burrow celebrated his first NFL touchdown with his teammates. But the Bengals still lost the game. The next week, they lost to the Cleveland Browns. Then Cincinnati tied the Philadelphia Eagles. Going up against the Jacksonville Jaguars in his fourth NFL game, Burrow was hungry for a win.

With the Bengals behind by seven points in the second quarter, Burrow drove his team down the field. He threw a short pass to teammate Joe Mixon. Mixon raced to the end zone. Touchdown!

The Bengals kept scoring. They beat Jacksonville 33–25 for Burrow's first NFL win. The team had a long way to go to reach their final goal: the Super Bowl. But Burrow was happy to get his first victory. "We got the win, that's all I care about," he said. "It feels good to win. I'm going to do whatever it takes to win football games."

JOE COOL

Joe playing for Athens High School in 2014

Joe Burrow was born in Ames, Iowa, on December 10, 1996. He lived with his family in Fargo, North Dakota. When Joe was eight, they moved to Athens County, Ohio.

As a senior in high school, Joe threw 62 touchdowns passes and just two interceptions.

Joe's family was full of football players. His father, Jim, played for the Green Bay Packers in 1976. Then he played six seasons in the Canadian Football League. Joe's older brothers, Dan and Jamie, played college football at the University of Nebraska.

Joe began playing football in third grade. His coaches called him Joe Cool. Head coach Sam Smathers made Joe the team's quarterback. "We were in the championship game his first year," Smathers said. "We won it the second year."

At Athens High School, Joe played basketball and football. He was one of the best point guards in Ohio. But he was even better at football. In 2014, he won the Mr. Football award as the best player in the state. He graduated from Athens in 2015. In three seasons on the varsity team, Joe had thrown 157 touchdown passes and just 17 interceptions.

Burrow's high school stats made him popular with college coaches around the US. Coaches from schools in Nebraska, Oklahoma, and Michigan contacted him. But he told them that he had already chosen a college. He was going to Ohio State University.

In 2019, Burrow received a special honor. Officials at Athens High School gave their football stadium a new name: Joe Burrow Stadium.

Burrow playing for Ohio State in 2016

   Most star high school players don't start out being stars in college. Burrow sat on the bench for Ohio State's entire 2015 season. In 2016, he played in five games as the team's backup quarterback. He was the backup again the following year and played in five more games. Burrow had played well in his 10 college games. But if he wanted to be a starting quarterback, he would have to do it at a different school.

After the 2017 season, Burrow transferred to Louisiana State University (LSU). He started for LSU in 2018 and led the Tigers to a 10–3 record. His 16 touchdown passes and five interceptions were good enough to keep his job. But 2018 was just a warm-up to one of the greatest seasons in college football history.

Burrow, in his LSU uniform, celebrates in a game against the University of Miami.

Georgia Southern University was the first team LSU played in 2019. It took Burrow less than three minutes to throw his first touchdown of the season. He finished the game with an amazing five touchdown passes.

LSU crushed Georgia Southern 55–3. Then the Tigers beat Texas 45–38. LSU kept rolling, racking up win after win. On January 13, 2020, they played Clemson in the College Football Playoff National Championship. Clemson struck first with a touchdown. Then Burrow threw to teammate Ja'Marr Chase for a 52-yard score to tie the game.

Burrow throws a pass against Northwestern State in 2019.

Burrow's incredible last college season made him a popular pick for the 2020 NFL Draft.

Burrow threw five total touchdowns in the game to lead LSU to a 42–25 win. The Tigers were national champions! They finished the season with a perfect 15–0 record. Burrow's stats were shocking: 60 touchdown passes and just six interceptions. He won the Heisman Trophy, the award for college football's best player.

TIME TO WORK

Burrow playing in his first season with the Cincinnati Bengals in 2020.

The Bengals had one big advantage after finishing in last place in 2019. They got to choose first in the 2020 NFL Draft. Many fans expected the team to pick Burrow.

Players, their families, and NFL officials usually meet for the draft. But in 2020, the new disease COVID-19 affected people around the world. The NFL decided to hold the draft online to avoid spreading the disease.

When the draft took place in April, the Bengals didn't surprise anyone. They chose Burrow to be their next starting quarterback. The online event was a huge success. More than 55 million fans watched Burrow become a Bengal.

Those who watched the 2020 NFL Draft saw Burrow (center) at home with his parents when he was selected by the Bengals.

Burrow practices with dummies that act as defenders with their arms raised.

Bengals fans were excited. But they also wondered how good Burrow would be. Burrow just wanted to play. "Enough talk," he wrote on Twitter. "Time to get to work."

During the football season, Burrow is busy almost every day. To get ready for games, he practices, learns new plays, and meets with coaches. As the season goes on, all the work and exercise cause Burrow to lose weight. In the off-season, he tries to add weight to his body.

Burrow was ready to work in the 2020 off-season. But the Bengals had shut down to avoid spreading COVID-19. They canceled many team workouts. Burrow would have to start preparing for his first NFL season without the team's help.

That summer, Burrow met with some of his teammates. The players lifted weights in the gym. By July, Burrow was bigger and stronger than he had been at the draft.

Burrow (left) celebrates with teammates after scoring his first touchdown for the Bengals.

Burrow (*right*) with some of his teammates before the start of the 2020 season

The NFL reopened in early August so players could get ready for the season to start in September. They worked out and practiced together in small groups. Each group spent an hour in the weight room and an hour practicing on the field. As the start of the season drew nearer, the players spent more time practicing.

Burrow impressed his new teammates. He zipped the ball around the field with his powerful right arm. He felt confident. And he knew all the team's plays. "You can tell he's really worked hard at it in the off-season," said Bengals wide receiver Alex Erickson.

FIGHTING HUNGER

Burrow is tackled by defensive end Derek Barnett of the Philadelphia Eagles in 2020.

Burrow spoke about hunger in his hometown as he accepted the 2019 Heisman Trophy.

The 2019 Heisman Trophy ceremony took place in New York City in December.

When Burrow was announced as the winner, he stood and hugged his friends, family, and coaches. Then he walked to the stage and gave a special speech.

Burrow talked from his heart about his life and football career. He also had a message for people in his hometown. "I'm up here for all those kids in Athens and

Athens County that go home to not a lot of food on the table, hungry after school," he said. "You guys can be up here too."

Burrow's speech inspired people to help others. Some gave money to the Athens County Food Pantry. The pantry provides free food to people who might go hungry without it. Within a month, people inspired by Burrow's speech had given more than $500,000 to the group.

In 2020, Burrow and the Athens County Food Pantry created the Joe Burrow Hunger Relief Fund. The fund will provide food support for people in the Athens County area for years.

Burrow loves SpongeBob SquarePants. He often wears clothes that include images from the show. He wore SpongeBob SquarePants socks to the 2019 Heisman Trophy ceremony.

Home Again

Burrow earns millions of dollars from the Bengals. But during the **COVID-19** shutdown in 2020, he lived with his parents. He stayed in his old bedroom. The room still had his *Star Wars* posters on the walls.

Burrow said he felt as if he were in high school again. He watched *The Office* and other TV shows with his dad. He played video games in the basement. He played catch with hometown friends. Burrow joked that he even had to ask his parents for permission to go to the grocery store.

A poster for the movie *Star Wars: A New Hope*

TIME TO HEAL

Burrow readies a pass in a November 2020 game against the Washington Football Team.

Burrow's goal was to make Cincinnati a winning team. But after beating Jacksonville for his first NFL win, the Bengals lost four of their next five games.

Burrow was seriously injured in the game against Washington, taking him out for the rest of the season.

On November 22, 2020, Cincinnati played the Washington Football Team. After a touchdown pass from Burrow, the Bengals led 9–7. In the second half, he stepped back to make a pass. As he threw the ball, a Washington defender crashed into his legs.

Burrow's left knee twisted and bent. He fell to the field in pain. The knee was badly injured, and Burrow's season was finished. On December 2, he had surgery to repair the damage.

Food banks experienced high demand during the COVID-19 pandemic as many lost their incomes.

Bengals fans were crushed. To show support for their star player, many began giving money to the Joe Burrow Hunger Relief Fund. Some fans gave $9 gifts in honor of Burrow's jersey number. In just a couple of days, fans donated almost $30,000 to the fund.

Doctors expect Burrow to take about a year to fully recover from his injury. With surgery behind him, he can focus on healing and getting stronger. He began throwing a football about two months after surgery. "The worst part is over, and the fun part begins," he said. Burrow can't wait to get back on the field to help make the Bengals a winning team.

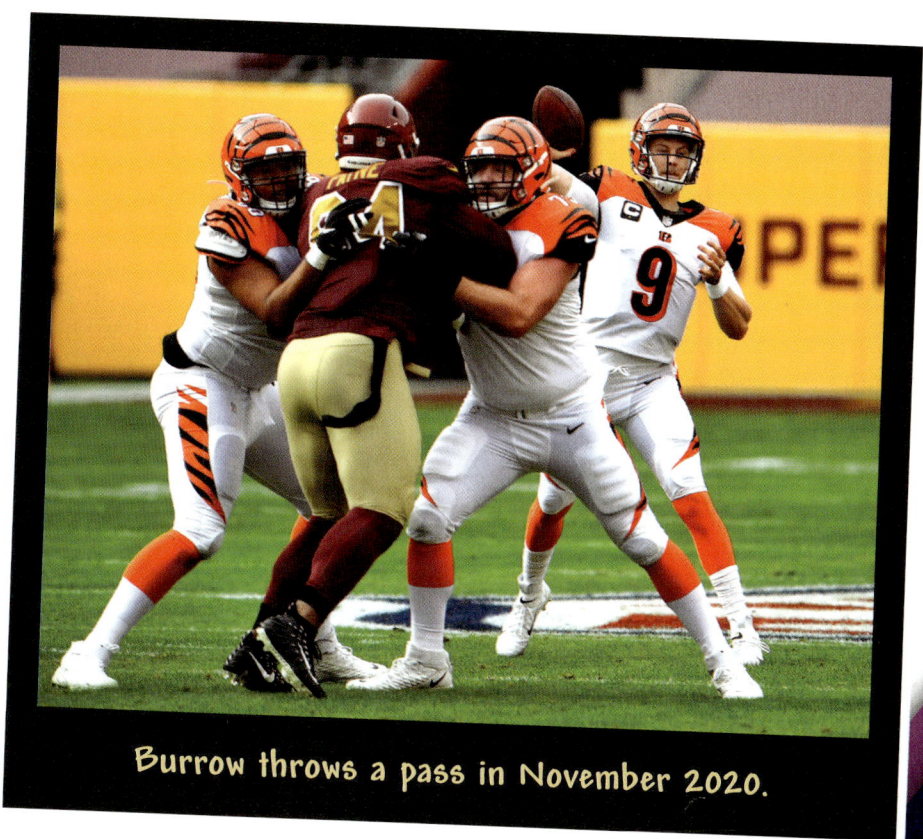

Burrow throws a pass in November 2020.

Player	Touchdown passes	Year
1. Joe Burrow	60	2019
2. Colt Brennan	58	2006
3. David Klingler	54	1990
4. B. J. Symons	52	2003
5. Dwayne Haskins	50	2018
Derek Carr	50	2013
Sam Bradford	50	2008
8. Brandon Doughty	49	2014

Glossary

backup: a person who takes the place of or supports another

end zone: the area at each end of a football field where players score touchdowns

Heisman Trophy: an award given each year to the best player in college football

interception: a pass caught by the defending team that results in a change of possession

off-season: the part of a year when a sports league is inactive

point guard: the player who leads a basketball team on offense

start: to be in the lineup at the beginning of a game

transfer: to leave a school and enroll at another

varsity: the top team at a school

Source Notes

7 Glen West, "Former LSU Quarterback Joe Burrow Notches First NFL Win in Record Setting Fashion," *Sports Illustrated*, October 4, 2020, https://www.si.com/college/lsu/football/joe-burrow-first-career-win.

9 Branson Wright, "'An Example of Humanity': Athens County Knows Social Awareness Is Nothing New for LSU Quarterback Joe Burrow," *Cleveland.com*, updated January 4, 2020, https://www.cleveland.com/news/2019/12/an-example-of-humanity-athens-county-knows-social-awareness-is-nothing-new-for-lsu-quarterback-joe-burrow.html.

17 Allen Kim, "Bengals Select Joe Burrow with the First Pick in the 2020 NFL Draft," CNN, April 24, 2020, https://www.cnn.com/2020/04/23/us/2020-nfl-draft-spt-trnd/index.html.

19 Kevin Patra, "Bengals Players Rave about Joe Burrow as Workouts Begin," NFL, August 7, 2020, https://www.nfl.com/news/bengals-players-rave-about-joe-burrow-as-workouts-begin.

21–22 Billy Witz, "As Joe Burrow Spoke of Hunger, His Hometown Felt the Lift," *New York Times*, January 13, 2020, https://www.nytimes.com/2020/01/13/sports/as-joe-burrow-spoke-of-hunger-his-hometown-felt-the-lift.html.

27 Ben Baby, "Cincinnati Bengals QB Joe Burrow Hopes to Begin Throwing in February as He Recovers from Knee Surgery," *ESPN*, January 12, 2021, https://www.espn.com/nfl/story/_/id/30699165/cincinnati-bengals-qb-joe-burrow-hopes-begin-throwing-february-recovers-knee-surgery.

Learn More

Bailey, Diane. *The Story of the Cincinnati Bengals*. Minneapolis: Kaleidoscope, 2020.

Cooper, Robert. *LSU Tigers*. Minneapolis: Abdo, 2021.

Football—*Sports Illustrated Kids*
https://www.sikids.com/football

Joe Burrow—Heisman Trophy
https://www.heisman.com/heisman-winners/joe-burrow/

Joe Burrow—NFL
https://www.nfl.com/players/joe-burrow/

Monson, James. *Behind the Scenes Football*. Minneapolis: Lerner Publications, 2020.

Index

Athens, OH, 8, 10, 21–22

Cincinnati Bengals, 4–7, 15–19, 23–27

food pantry, 22

Heisman Trophy, 14, 21–22

injury, 5, 27

Louisiana State University (LSU), 12–14

Ohio State University, 10–11

practice, 17, 19

touchdown, 5–7, 10, 12–14, 25

win, 4, 7, 9, 13–14, 21, 24, 27

Photo Acknowledgments

Image credits: AP Photo/Kyle Ross/Icon Sportswire, pp. 4–5, 15; AP Photo/Ian Johnson/Icon Sportswire, p. 6; AP Photo/Scott W. Grau/Icon Sportswire, pp. 8, 9; AP Photo/Jay LaPrete, p. 11; AP Photo/Aaron M. Sprecher, p. 12; AP Photo/Patrick Dennis, pp. 13, 14; AP Photo/NFL, p. 16; AP Photo/Aaron Doster, p. 17; AP Photo/Bryan Woolston, pp. 18, 19; AP Photo/Andy Lewis/Icon Sportswire, p. 20; AP Photo/Jason Szenes, p. 21; AF archive/Alamy Stock Photo, p. 23; AP Photo/Randy Litzinger/Icon Sportswire, pp. 24, 25, 27; AP Photo/Paul Hennessy/NurPhoto, p. 26.

Cover image: AP Photo/Albert Tielemans.